For W

GW00838718

Terry Scope's
Telescope

from Memememe

Jnkerr

by

Jonkers

(www.writtenbyjonkers.co.uk)

Illustrated by

Henryk Jachimczyk

(www.henthepen.co.uk)

Grosvenor House
Publishing Limited

The right of Jonkers to be identified as the author of this
work has been asserted by him in accordance with Section 78
of the Copyright, Designs and Patents Act 1988

The book cover picture is copyright to Jonkers

This book is published by
Grosvenor House Publishing Ltd
28-30 High Street, Guildford, Surrey, GU1 3EL.
www.grosvenorhousepublishing.co.uk

A CIP record for this book
is available from the British Library

ISBN 978-1-78148-388-6

Also by Jonkers:

Jimpy

William Hockley

Contents

Contents

Chapter 1

My Hilarious Parents

You might say that my parents had (or have) a sense of humour. I would not say this. If your surname is Head, you do not call your child Dick (or Richard). If your surname is Down, you do not call your son Neil. If your surname is King, you do not call your sons Lee or Joe.

"Are you Lee King?"

"Yes sir."

"Then wipe it up!"

"And you. Are you Joe King?"

"No, I'm deadly serious sir!"

Ha, ha, ha. Not!

My father's surname (and as it turns out my mother's too) is Scope. Now you wouldn't think there'd be a lot of 'scope' (apologies for the pun) for names that would look, and sound, silly with the surname. But they managed it! My brother (he's 5 years older than me) was named Perry. Perry Scope (as in those things used in submarines to keep watch above water). Obviously that one is spelt 'periscope' but it still sounds the same. 'Up Periscope' was always the chant they used at him, especially when he was swimming. Or 'Stick your head out the door and see if the teacher's coming Perry Scope'. He hated school. He's nineteen now and works. He has not joined the Navy.

My name? It's Terry. Terry Scope. Try saying that again. And again. Terry Scope, Terry Scope. Try it with a Chinese accent. Exactly! Telescope. Even if people shorten my name to Tel (as some do), my middle name is Edward so I become Tel E Scope. There's no escaping it, and trust me I've tried, my name always sounds like Telescope.

"Look at Terry Scope gazing into space again."

"I reckon you'll be a 'star' one day Terry Scope."

"Are you looking at Uranus?"

Ha, ha, ha. Not!! For the second time! I hate school too. One of these stupid comments actually came from a teacher! Rich coming from her too, considering that she is called Miss Take. It was certainly a 'Miss Take' when Mr and Mrs Take decided to have a child (in my opinion).

The thing is, despite all the stick that I've received because of my name, I have always been fascinated by astronomy. I'm 14 now but have been obsessed with the stars, planets, the Moon and space since I could read or look at pictures in a book. I've now got a Zestron Star SX80 telescope! That may not mean much to you. Let me just say that it's a serious bit of gear!!

That's where the whole thing started.

Chapter 2

Meeting a Moonbeam

It was a clear night. The stars were out (but they'd soon be back!) and the Moon was full. Terry poured himself a Coke, settled down into his chair and readied the telescope. This is where he spent most of his Friday nights (and often early Saturday mornings). He was lucky enough to have his room in the loft and his dad had actually put in an extra-large sky light and a special platform for his telescope. His dad wasn't all bad.

Terry had only had the Zestron Star SX80 for about 3 days so it was all pretty new to him and everything was much more detailed and clearer than his old telescope. It was great! Delphinius, Pegasus, Cygnus; at least that's what the book said. He may be obsessed but he was no expert. As he says 'it's not as easy as you may think'. And the Moon! He'd never seen it in such close detail.

As midnight passed, then 1a.m his eyes were starting to struggle. Reluctantly he gave in. Terry hadn't realised that he'd actually been getting quite cold just sitting there, so it felt good to slide under the covers. Very quickly he was completely zonked; but not for long.

He was woken by a knocking at the skylight. He half opened his eyes then slumped back down. It tapped again; louder this time. He rubbed his eyes. What on earth was it? A bird? A cat? The wind? Santa come 3 months early? It continued, louder and louder. Terry looked up. And there it was! What it was he had no idea, but THERE IT WAS!!

Its face was squashed flat against the glass and its arms and legs were stretched out like a four-legged starfish. It was roughly the size of a twelve month old baby. Terry couldn't tell if it was wearing any clothes or not; everything just seemed to merge together and there were no noticeable 'dangly bits' or holes to be seen. The whole thing, apart from the head (I'll talk about that in a minute), was an orangey colour, similar to the ridiculous fake tans that so many of the girls in Terry's class used. Now the head! Bright, almost blinding, glowing orange; large and round; very round with tiny, black eyes, no noticeable ears, a thin, black mouth, dead straight from one side of the face to the other and no nose.

Terry wanted to run, but couldn't. He just stared in disbelief. His legs had turned, not into jelly, but concrete. Suddenly *it* raised an arm and slammed hard onto the glass. Terry's legs recovered. He shot back and dived under the bed. Unfortunately his bed has drawers underneath so he just whacked his head, hard! Rubbing his head, Terry risked another peek at the skylight. He wished he hadn't. He'd forgotten to close it. The 'thing' was squeezing through the narrow gap. Terry cowered back against his bedside cabinet. It was through! It was in his room!

With its hands somehow sticking to the ceiling, it pulled itself towards Terry until it was almost directly above him. Its face stared down at him and the eyes slowly widened until they covered nearly half the face. It was hard to read its expression but Terry was sure it wasn't happy. The mouth started to widen...

"What on Earth do you think you're doing?" it boomed. "How would you like it?"

Terry was too dumbstruck to answer back.

"Night after night; hour upon hour; staring, always staring!"

"Who... are.... you?" Terry finally managed to ask.

"Me? I'm sure you know that, you've never stopped looking at us since you were a little kid. And now you've got that thing," he said, pointing at the Zestron Star SX80. "So nosy!"

"But, what...? Who or what are you?"

"I am a Moonling and my name is Momomomomo Moonbeam."

"A what? Who?"

"I said, I am a Moonling and my name is Momomomomo Moonbeam."

"Momomomo Moonbeam?"

"No, Momomomomo Moonbeam. Are you stupid as well as nosy?"

"Well it's a stupid name!"

"Look who's talking."

"How do you know my name?"

"We're not as stupid as Earth Folk you know. We know everyone. Anyway, I haven't come all this way just for a little chat. You are going to stop staring at us. You can keep looking at the stupid stars if you like but you will stop looking at us!"

"I've never seen you before in my life. Trust me, I'd remember someone as weird looking as you."

"Weird? Me? An Earthling daring to call a Moonling weird! You really are a most peculiar race. The fact remains that you have been watching our home for years and it must stop, or else!"

"Or else wh..?"

Terry scanned the room. He was alone. Where...?

"Are you alright up there? Who are you talking too? You on the phone? You need to get to bed."

"Ok dad."

Terry went to bed. He did not sleep. Or did he? Had he been asleep and dreamt the whole thing? He must have; how could it be anything else?

Chapter 3

More Moonbeams

Saturday evening. Terry had been on edge all day but he was determined not to let some crazy dream, no matter how real it seemed, stop him from his stargazing. It was another near perfect evening with just a few clouds scattered around the night sky. He positioned the telescope and used the moon as his first point of focus. It was particularly bright tonight.

'Boom! Thump, Thump!' Terry nearly fell off his chair as a strange little being with a large plate-like head suddenly appeared against the glass of the skylight. Before Terry could move, it had slipped through the skylight and, seemingly floating in mid-air, was looking down at him with tiny, piercing eyes. Its orange body seemed to glow in the dark.

"We warned you!"

"Don't hurt me... is this a dream? A nightmare?"

"It will become a nightmare if you don't stop staring at us!"

"So you're real?"

"Of course I'm real."

"So you really are a Moonling called Momomomomo?"

"No."

"No?"

"No, I'm a Moonling called Mamamamama. Momomomomo is my brother."

"This is crazy!"

"You were warned." With that the Moonling pointed a stubby finger towards the telescope which rose up, floated in mid-air, then vanished.

"What...? Stop! Give that back. You can't..."

But the Moonling was gone, and so was the telescope! Terry looked at where the telescope had been. His beloved Zestron Star SX80. He couldn't believe what had just happened. He pinched himself. "Ouch." He didn't pinch himself again. This was no dream. It should be. It had to be. But it wasn't!

Despite everything that had happened though, Moonlings, Momomomomo's, Mamamamama's and all, Terry was mostly worried about what his dad would say, or do, when he discovered that the brand new, expensive telescope he'd recently bought him had mysteriously vanished.

Terry didn't think his dad would believe the truth. *He* didn't believe the truth!

Chapter 4

Jambo

Terry made a decision. He phoned his best friend, Jambo and arranged to go round to his home on the following Friday to stargaze with him. If the same thing happened again at least he wouldn't be alone. It made sense. He could also borrow one of Jambo's old telescopes and sneak it into his own room. As long as there was a telescope of some description his dad probably wouldn't notice, not that he often went into Terry's room. Just in case though.

The night was not as clear as the previous week's, but there were still enough breaks in the cloud to satisfy the boys. Terry made a point of aiming directly at the Moon for quite some time but there was no sign of any Moonlings or any strange happenings. Perhaps it was all in his mind. Relieved, he slipped into his bed and Jambo climbed into his. After a bit of a chat about Miss Mullen's (the P.E teacher) legs and other promi- nent parts of her body, and a 10 minute farting compe- tition (which Jambo won comfortably), they both fell fast asleep.

Saturday evening. Terry had decided that he'd use Jambo's spare telescope, partly because he wanted to and partly so that his dad didn't grow suspicious and wonder why he'd suddenly lost interest in stargazing. The telescope wasn't nearly as good as the Zestron Star SX80 and the sky was a bit cloudy so Terry flopped across his bed, flicking through his 'Book of Astronomy and Space'. Very soon, the book had dropped onto his chest and little snoring noises were coming from his nose.

"Terry. Terry! Terry!!"

"Uh?"

"Terry, it's Mrs Jessop on the phone. James (Jambo) isn't up there with you is he?"

"No, why?"

"Any idea where he might be?"

"No. I haven't seen him since I left this morning. What's up?"

"Can you just have a quick word...?"

Jambo's mum was clearly in a panic. 'James' had gone up to his room at about nine o'clock but when she'd gone to see him at about a quarter to eleven, she couldn't find him anywhere. She hadn't heard him come down; there was no note or anything. She was scared. It was as if he'd just vanished!

Chapter 5

Basil

Vanished? Terry pondered, then pondered some more. Could it be…? No, there must be a simple explanation. Perhaps he'd run away for some reason. Not like Jambo though, definitely not like Jambo.

By lunchtime there was still no news. Mrs Jessop had phoned the police and Terry and his mum had gone round to see if there was anything they could do. Mrs Jessop took them up to Jambo's room where Terry immediately noticed that something was wrong; it was the telescope. It had a really obvious bend in it. Terry looked closer. How could that have happened? The lens was broken as well. He looked through it but couldn't see a thing.

"What's wrong Terry?" Mrs J asked.

"It's broken. The lens is smashed and the telescope has been bent right out of shape."

"Broken…? You don't reckon that's…?"

"It's possible," chipped in my Mum, "perhaps he was worried he'd get into trouble and ran off. It's a thought."

There continued a great deal of discussion about this and the possible whereabouts of Jambo. Terry was questioned about places he might have run off to, friends he had, had the telescope been alright yesterday? Had he been in a strange mood? And so on, and so on and so on. Terry answered as best he could but his mind kept wandering. It was really nagging him. The broken lens he could understand, just. But the bend in the telescope was another matter, another matter entirely. How could it bend like that? It was pretty solid, and even if Jambo had for some bizarre reason decided to whack it against a wall or something, it still wouldn't have bent in such a smooth curvature. There were no obvious dents, no marks at all. Something was wrong; something was very wrong! Terry wondered. Momomomomo? Mamamamama? Moonlings? No! It couldn't be...! Could it?

The day went and the evening came. Still no sign of Jambo. By now the Jessops were seriously concerned. There'd been no sightings and nothing for the police to go on. Nothing seemed to have gone from Jambo's room; except Jambo.

Midnight came. Terry was up in his room but couldn't sleep. Vanished? Moonlings? Crazy...but... He quietly closed the hatch to his room and sat down in front of his telescope; Jambo's telescope. The moon was bright. Slowly he pulled the telescope around and focused it on the moon. Almost immediately there was a loud thud on the glass of the skylight. A Moonling had landed. This had to be real! It couldn't be, but it had to be!

The orange body and large, bright-orange face looked down at him, then squeezed through the gap in the skylight.

"So, are you Momomomomo Moonbeam or Mamamamama Moonbeam?"

"Neither."

"No?"

"No."

"Don't tell me," he said sarcastically, "you're Mimimimimi Moonbeam or perhaps Mumumumumu Moonbeam or..."

"No."

"Who are you then?"

"Basil."

"Basil?"

"No, not really, just kidding! I'm Me!"

"What do you mean, you're *me*?"

"I'm Me."

"No. I'm me and you are you."

"No. You are you and I am Me."

"Yes, I am me but who are you?"

"I am Me."

"Look stop! Just stop! This is ridiculous!"

"My name is Me, it's short for Mememememe."

"Oh? What do you want? What have you done with my friend?"

"You have a friend?"

"Very funny!" What have you done with him?"

"I don't know what you're talking about. I'm here to watch you."

"What do you mean, watch me?"

"You were warned, twice. Still you keep staring at us. We can't keep warning you so now we're going to watch *you*."

"What do you mean 'watch me'?"

"You'll see. For now I must go."

"But what about Jambo? What have you done to him? Where is he?"

"Would that be your friend whose telescope you've been using to stare at us again?"

"Yes."

"I have no idea where he is. Goodbye."

"But…"

It was too late. Mememememe had gone, for now.

Chapter 6

Under Moonling Watch

Jambo was still missing. It had now been four days. There were no new leads, in fact no leads at all. The Jessops had made a heartfelt plea on the News; the police had widened their search but still no sightings; not even 'possible' sightings. The fear was now growing. Mr and Mrs Jessop were beside themselves (literally and metaphorically). Terry was expected to continue as normal; go to school, do his homework, eat. He didn't want to do any of these things. Then things got worse, much worse.

It first happened as he was going to the toilet at school. He was alone in the cubicle when he suddenly heard a strange voice from above. He looked up to see one of the Moonlings looking down at him.

"We're watching you. Don't forget to wipe your bottom and wash your hands."

It disappeared.

In class, he was attempting some Maths work when suddenly a Moonling appeared, grabbed his pencil and threw it in the general direction of the teacher. It missed, but was noticed. He received a detention. Clearly nobody else had seen the Moonling. Was it only him who could see them or was he just seeing them in his mind? He really didn't know what to think any more.

He would be watching television, when a Moonling's head would suddenly appear from above or around the side of it. He'd be eating his dinner when a Moonling would make itself comfortable right in the middle of the table, leaning back on the vase. They never even let him rest at night. Sometimes there was more than one. He could hear them talking in the dark. He'd tried closing the skylight but they still managed to get in somehow. Sometimes they wouldn't appear for hours only for one to suddenly materialise when least expected, scaring Terry out of his skin. He was becoming a wreck. His parents had noticed but just put it down to him worrying about Jambo. He couldn't tell them anything different, they'd think he'd gone nuts. Perhaps he had!

Everything was to come to a head on a Sunday morning when Terry and his parents had gone to church. They were holding a special service for the Jessops and praying for the safe return of their son. As Terry opened his eyes from praying, one of the Moonlings suddenly appeared directly in front of him, standing upright on the back of the pew in front of him. It was too much. He screamed.

"Get away! Get away! Leave me alone!" He stood up and ran out of the church, his worried parents following him.

"Terry, Terry love, what's wrong?"

"I don't know mum, I don't know what's happening to me."

"Is it Jambo?" his dad asked gently.

"Partly, but..."

"What is it? You can tell us?"

"But it's crazy."

"Just tell us."

"I keep seeing things."

"What kind of things?"

"Moonlings."

"Moonlings?"

"I told you it was crazy."

He then went on to tell them the whole story. Either they'd believe him or they'd help him; at the moment he didn't care which. He just wanted the Moonlings, real or imaginary, to leave him alone.

Chapter 7

Talk to me Terry

They didn't believe him. Who would? They nodded, they smiled, they patted him on the head and they even cuddled him (dad as well!) but they didn't believe him. His mum had even started crying when he'd told them about Momomomomo, Mamamamama and Mememememe. They decided that Terry should 'talk' to somebody; a professional. In short, he was going to see a psychologist; a specialist child psychologist. It was official then, thought Terry, he was definitely at least four sandwiches short of a picnic, three crème eggs short of a dozen, five playing cards short of a full deck, he was as nutty as a pile of squirrel droppings, he was...(Oh, you get the picture). He was actually a little relieved. At least something was going to be done. At least he'd get some help. But of course that was before he met Jeremy!

"Hello, you must be Terry," he said as he advanced towards Terry and his mum. As there was only Terry and his mum in the waiting room, Terry was less than impressed that Jeremy was able to pick him out. They'd given their names at reception and anyway, the appointment had been made last week.

"Please come through Terry. Do you mind if I call you Terry?"

Terry shook his head. 'What else are you going to call me?' he thought, 'Bill?' This really wasn't a very promising start. Terry was not exactly warming to Jeremy.

"Mummy will be just outside while we have a friendly little chat."

'Mummy!!! Mummy!!!' Terry wanted to shout, 'I'm 14 years old not 3!" He looked back despairingly at his mum as he went through to the other room. He was worried that part of the therapy might be being forced to watch Teletubbies or play Pat-a-cake, Pat-a-cake with Jeremy. He'd rather keep seeing Moonlings all over the place!

"That's right, take a seat, well don't actually take it!" laughed Jeremy in an attempt to lighten the mood. It failed. 'Save me' thought Terry.

"Now then, I want you to tell me all about these strange creatures you've been seeing lately. Take your time, just start when you're ready."

Terry was far from sure that he wanted to tell this man anything. He looked over to him and took in the silly goatee beard, the red, flared jeans and the brown sandals, not to mention the ponytail (sorry, I've mentioned it now). 'What a plank!' he thought.

For five minutes – that seemed like hours – Terry just sat there while Jeremy sat back in his chair and smiled at him, occasionally tilting his head to one side and lifting his eyebrows in what Terry assumed was an effort to encourage him to start talking. It didn't work. Another five minutes passed. Still neither of them spoke. Eventually the quiet started getting to Terry and he suddenly blurted out, "I see Moonlings. They're little people that come from the Moon and one was called Mamamamama, another was called Momomomomo and another was called Mememememe and they don't like me staring at them and they came down to warn me and they must've got Jambo because he was looking at them too…." And so he continued in one very long, very fast sentence, never stopping for breath. Strangely it felt good to have got it all out. Jeremy waited for Terry to stop and said, "I see." He then settled back in his chair and waited for Terry to continue.

"And now they're watching me to get their own back and the other day one of them came down in class and…." He rattled off another long, rambling sentence without a pause.

"I see," said Jeremy.

Terry blurted out sentence after sentence after sentence with no breaks, no breaths and an increasing frustration with the lack of response he was getting from Jeremy.

"I see," Jeremy said again.

Time was up. That was the full half hour.

"Thank you Terry. Thank you for telling me."

"Is that it?"

"Yes."

"So?"

"What?"

"Am I nuts?"

"Not a term we like to use Terry."

"Alright, is there something wrong with me?"

"What do you think?"

"I don't know, that's why I've come to see you!"

"Is it?"

"Yes, but you just keep answering all my questions with another question."

"Do I?"

"You just did it again!"

"Did I?"

"And again!"

"Sorry, is it annoying you?"

"Yes! And that's another question! You're doing my head in!"

"Am I?"

"Yes!!!!"

"I see."

"Aaaagh!!"

Terry hurried to the door and rushed over to his mum. He grabbed her as she stood up and held her tight. He was extremely agitated. Jeremy strolled casually towards them.

"Aah, Mrs Scope, that was a very useful session. Terry's been very helpful."

"Oh good. Do you think you'll be able to help him?"

"Does Terry?" he asked back, looking patronisingly towards him. Terry remained tight-lipped.

"I think it would be a great help if I were to visit Terry at home and perhaps he could show me where he does his stargazing. Perhaps we'll even get to see some of the Moonlings," he said with a sly wink to his mother.

"I'm sure that would be great, wouldn't it Terry?" Terry just cried. Could things get any worse? Well, yes they could. MUCH WORSE!

Chapter 8

What's Worse Than Being Abducted?

There was a knock on the door. Terry winced. It was Friday night, 9 o'clock, Jeremy had arrived.

"Terry, Jeremy's here, can you come down please? Terry, can you hear me? Terry!"

Terry knew there was no point in ignoring his mum or trying to make a jump for it out of the bedroom window. Even so, it was very tempting. He took a deep breath and climbed down from his room. Jeremy was waiting in the hall; big, patronising grin already fixed in place.

"Hi ya mate." He held out his hand. Terry shook it weakly. 'Hi ya mate indeed' he thought to himself. No mate of mine! Reluctantly, Terry showed Jeremy up to his room.

"So, this is your den then!"

"No. It's my room."

"And this must be where you do the old stargazing."

Once more Terry was impressed by Jeremy's amazing powers of deduction. Perhaps the telescope had given it away.

"Yes."

"And this is where the Moonlings come in?" he asked, pointing up to the skylight.

"Yes."

"And have they visited you this week at all? Here, at school, anywhere else?"

"Yes."

"Here?"

"Yes."

"Can you tell me anything about it?"

"No."

As you may have guessed by the conversation so far, Terry was not being hugely co-operative. He had decided to talk to Jeremy as little as possible and only to give simple monosyllabic answers. You could take a boy to a 'shrink' but you couldn't make him talk!

"Do you mind if I have a look?"

"No."

This short, very short, answer was to have very grave consequences. Almost as soon as Jeremy had spun the telescope round to point out of the skylight and began to focus it on the moon, there was a loud thud above him. He looked up. He jolted backwards and fell off his seat, crashing into Terry's wardrobe. For the first time in a while, Terry laughed. He laughed out loud. Jeremy didn't move. Terry laughed even louder. Jeremy still didn't move. Terry looked closer at him. Was he dead? Suddenly it wasn't so funny. He still laughed though!

"Who's he?" came a voice from above.

Terry looked up and there was one of the Moonlings. So that was why he'd fallen off the chair, Jeremy had seen it too.

"Just someone… What are you doing here?"

"You were looking at us again."

"I wasn't. *He* was."

"Even so, it's *your* telescope and it's *your* room and it's *your* friend."

"Friend! Friend? Trust me, he's no friend of mine."

"He'll have to come too."

"Come where? What are you talking about?"

"I think you call it an abduction. You're coming with us. You and your friend."

"For the last time, he's not my friend! Did you abduct Jambo?"

"Jambo? Who's that?"

"You have, haven't you? His parents are worried sick. Bring him back... you're..."

"I don't have a clue what you're talking about. Anyway it's time to go."

"Abduct me then! I don't care, but please bring Jambo back and please, please, please, and more pleases, don't bring Jeremy as well. I could cope with being abducted but not with Jeremy. Please!"

"Sorry. He's seen us."

Suddenly Terry could feel himself floating. He was also very sleepy.

Two hours later, Mr Scope knocked on the hatch to Terry's room. There was no answer. He pushed it open. He looked round. He looked round again. And again. He kept looking. He searched all the other rooms. He looked everywhere but... THEY WEREN'T THERE!

Chapter 9

Moon Landing

They weren't there because they were on the Moon. That's right, the Moon. It had taken about twenty seconds from Terry's room to landing on the Moon. Just how that had happened, Terry had no idea. He hadn't been able to see properly when they were being abducted, but he thought that he (and Jeremy!) had been sucked up into some kind of vessel. It was only now that they had landed, Terry could see a little bit more. They seemed to be inside a sort of glass sphere. Apart from Jeremy, Terry and the Moonling, the dome was completely empty. Terry was actually rather disappointed. He wanted to see lots of electronic dials, flashing lights, computers; he wanted Star Trek or Star Wars. What he got was little more than a giant gerbil ball. There weren't even any seats. That was just about the only thing that was of any real interest to Terry. If there were no seats, then why were they not thrown about all over the dome? They had just stayed completely still despite the fact that the globe, dome, or whatever it was must have travelled incredibly quickly. They didn't even touch the sides, they just seemed to float. Weird! Oh, and of course one other thing that pricked Terry's interest just slightly was that they were now sitting inside a glass (or some other clear material) dome on the Moon. The Moon!!! THE MOON!!!!

Jeremy was beginning to wake up, to Terry's great disappointment.

"What...? Where?"

"On the Moon."

"On the Moon? Oh, Terry, what's going on young man?"

"We're on the Moon. We've been abducted by Moonlings. We've..."

"Now, now Terry, we know that's not possible... The skylight! That thing!"

"Aaahh, so your memory's starting to come back is it?"

"There he is!" Jeremy shouted in disbelief and trepidation.

"She," corrected the Moonling. I'm a *she*, if you don't mind."

"Where are we? Who are you? Are you real? What's going on?"

"He asks a lot of questions doesn't he?"

"Don't I know it!" Terry agreed.

"Ok, time to disembark."

"But we can't just go out there!" Terry bawled out in alarm, "We won't be able to breathe. We have to wear space suits and stuff."

"Only if you were going *on* the Moon."

"But we are, aren't we?"

"Of course we're not, have you seen it? Oh, stupid question, of course you've seen it, you spend nearly every weekend staring at it. Not much to see is there? A few craters and a load of dust."

"So where are we going then?"

"In the Moon."

"In the Moon? What do you mean*, in* the Moon*?"*

"In. Inside. Do you know, we used to think that we were inferior to Humans and that you were 'intelligent beings'." She started laughing. "Can you imagine, you, Human Beings, intelligent!" She was almost bursting she was laughing so much.

Once she'd regained some of her composure, she pressed her hand against the side of the dome. The floor opened up beneath them and they fell gently downwards through a gap in the Moon's crust. They came to rest on a circular platform seemingly suspended in mid-air. They looked down upon what appeared to be a large town or city. Terry couldn't help thinking that it looked very much like an aerial view of a town or city on Earth. There were numerous buildings and some kind of vehicles moving around what seemed to be roads. It was hard to see individual Moonlings but Terry assumed that the little dots moving about so far below were exactly that. If so, there were thousands; maybe millions!

Terry couldn't help feeling a bit cheated. All that time he'd spent studying the Moon and everything that was really *interesting* was *inside*. No wonder Moonlings thought Humans were stupid. He *felt* stupid; night after night staring at some great big lump of rock with a few far from interesting craters on it!

The platform slowly began to spin and drop. The buildings gradually became larger and the roads and vehicles clearer. It still looked very much like Earth. Terry looked over at Jeremy. Jeremy was quiet. Jeremy was vacant. Jeremy was dumbstruck! 'At least he's a bit less annoying like that,' thought Terry.

As they got ever closer to the ground, Terry could see a large sign. There was a large 'M' and he could make out the word 'Welcome'. 'Welcome to Moon...

Welcome to Moonchester'. That was it, 'Welcome to Moonchester'.

At last they came to rest on the ground.

"This way," called the Moonling.

They followed. Terry stared around him in amazement as he tried to keep up with the Moonling. Jeremy just plodded forward, staring in front of him like some kind of Zombie. Terry was almost wishing that Jeremy would come out of this trance-like state and start talking. Almost!

There were houses; there were shops; there were bus stops; there were street lights; there were zebra crossings; there were... Well, there was just about everything that you'd find on Earth. In fact, it really reminded Terry of somewhere he'd been to but he couldn't think where. The only difference was that some of the places had slightly different names. There was a MoonDonalds restaurant, a Moon & Starbucks, both Tesco's and Sainsbury's Lunar stores, a Moon & Spencers and an F.K.C. There were also thousands of Moonlings bustling around. They all looked exactly the same to Terry; orange bodies, large, orange, plate-like heads, piercing black eyes and wide, thin mouths. They all seemed to be the same size too, roughly 60cm tall (or short).

The Moonling (just for the record she was called Mimamimami) led them on through the busy streets until she finally came to a stop outside a large, imposing building. She knocked on the door and waited. A buzzer buzzed (as is their job) and the huge, wooden door slowly swung open. Mimamimami looked back at Terry and Jeremy and ushered them inside.

Inside, the building was even more impressive than the exterior. Giant chandeliers hung down from the high ceiling, large paintings adorned the walls and the floor was made from hexagonal, light gold and cream marble tiles. 'Whoever lives here must be rich', thought Terry; very, very rich.

"You must wait here until you are called." With that, Mimamimami left the building, leaving Terry and Jeremy seated in the magnificent hallway. They waited and they waited. Terry grew increasingly nervous as time ticked on. Who were they waiting to see? What were they waiting for? Was it something good? (He doubted it). Was it something bad? (Much more likely).

"Jeremy. Jeremy. Jeremy! Can you hear me? Please speak to me." Terry was becoming desperate. He needed some form of company, someone to talk to... yes, even Jeremy!

"Is this really happening?" Jeremy asked.

"Yes."

"We're *inside* the Moon?"

"Yes."

"Really?"

"Don't start answering with questions again! Yes, we're inside the Moon, yes, we were abducted and yes Moonlings really exist! I can hardly believe it either but it wasn't all in my mind, this is REAL!"

"Groovy."

Just that one word was enough to make Terry wish that he hadn't encouraged Jeremy to talk. 'Groovy' indeed. Who on Earth (or on the Moon for that matter) still said 'groovy'?

Suddenly another Moonling appeared. "Come with me, he will see you now."

"Who?" asked Terry, not unreasonably.

"Who? Who? The Man in the Moon of course."

They followed the Moonling and were led into a large room. There, floating behind a huge black desk, legs and arms crossed and eyes closed was the Man in the Moon. He looked very similar to the Moonlings, with the same orange body and thin slits for eyes and mouth but his head was different; very different. It was at least three times the size of the Moonling's heads and instead of being flat and plate-like it was a huge sphere. His skin was very pitted and covered

in what looked like craters. It also looked very dry and dusty. He opened his eyes and stared at his visitors.

"Kneel!"

"No, Terry."

"And you can call me Jeremy."

"I said kneel!" boomed the Man in the Moon.

They knelt.

"You are a spy!" he cried, pointing at Terry. "And you!" he said pointing at Jeremy, "are just strange and extremely irritating!"

Terry couldn't help but be impressed by their sound knowledge of Jeremy but they hadn't done so well with the 'spy' thing.

"I'm not a spy!"

"Don't you dare question me! You are a spy. You've been watching us for months and months. We've seen you!"

"So you've been watching me too! That makes you a spy too then doesn't it?"

"Insolent Earthling! You dare to speak to the Man in the Moon in such a way? Do you know the trouble you're in? Do you know what the punishment is for spies?"

Terry didn't and didn't *want* to know. Somehow he knew that it wasn't going to be a severe telling off or a two-day grounding.

"Death. Death by hunging!"

"Hunging?"

"Yes, hunging. You will be hunged by the neck until dead!"

"Do you mean hanged?"

"If you keep questioning me I'll have you taken out and shoot instead."

"Don't you mean shot?"

"Take them away! Lock them up!"

Six Moonling guards suddenly appeared and grabbed Terry and Jeremy. They frog–or possibly toad–marched them out of the room, down some very steep steps and pushed them inside a dark, dingy cage. The door clanked behind them and the key was turned. They were trapped; imprisoned; they both knew that they were in grave danger. Soon they might just be *in* a grave!

Chapter 10

So, Where is Jambo?

"This is grave," said Terry, "very grave indeed".

"It is if we allow it to be," said Jeremy.

"What?"

"It's only a grave situation if we allow it to be. What we need to do is think positively, to see the positive aspects of our situation."

"Positive aspects? We're stuck in a cell or cage, it's dark, we're probably going to be hanged or shot, and to top it all I'm having to listen to you talking drivel."

"We're alive. We've got each other to talk to. It's an experience."

"An experience!!! Someone to talk to!!!! The only positive thing that I can think of is that at least if I'm hanged or shot, I won't have to listen to you again!"

"Now, now Terry, that's not very nice. You're stressed aren't you?"

"Brilliant!" said Terry, "You really are a fantastic psychologist."

"Thank you."

"A fantastic psychologist who has no understanding of sarcasm at all."

"Of what?"

"Look, we need to think. How do we get out of this mess?"

Before Jeremy could make any comment there was a sudden flurry of activity as a group of guards poured down the steps, halted outside the cell and opened the door.

"Move!"

They moved. The guards hurried them up the stairs and escorted them immediately into the Man In The Moon's office. His face had slightly waned since they had last seen him and was set with a very severe, stern expression. Terry feared the worse. Was this the end?

Suddenly, Jeremy threw himself to the ground and began to plead for his life.

"Please spare us oh Great One. I have a terrapin and a goldfish that depend on me. Who'll take care of them if I'm not there? Save Terry too, he's so young; think of the pain his parents are going through, think of his friends, his cousins. Please don't kill us, we'll do

42

anything you ask. We'll never look at the Moon again, we'll rid the Earth of telescopes, we'll fight for a law to ban astronomy, we'll do anything, just spare us."

"Shut up!" said the Man In The Moon bluntly.

Terry couldn't agree more. 'How embarrassing was that?' he thought to himself.

"We are not going to hung you or shot you now. There is a much more pressing problem that we need to address. It involves your friend."

"Who, Jambo?"

"Yes, Jambo."

"Where is he? Have you got him?"

"No, it's worse than that, much, much worse."

"He's not dead?"

"Not as far as we know. We have reliable information that suggests that he, like you, was abducted from Earth. Unfortunately for your friend, he was *not* abducted by Moonlings."

"Who then?"

"Urinals."

"Urinals?"

"Yes, Urinals. They live on the planet Urinal."

"Do you mean Uranus?"

"No, I don't mean my anus!! How dare you! I mean Urinals from the planet Urinal."

"There's no such planet."

"What would you know Earthling?" shouted the Man In The Moon angrily. "Have you honestly never seen a Urinal?"

"Of course I have."

"Where?"

"In the public toilets in Finchington; there's a whole row of them!"

"What are you talking about? The planet Urinal is closest to the planet that you used to call Pluto."

"But we'd have seen it."

"Of course you wouldn't! Really, you Earthlings must be the stupidest Beings in the galaxy! The planet Urinal is about the size of a pin head."

"A pin head? You're making it up. How could people live on a planet that size? I may be a human but I'm not completely stupid."

"Oh but you are. As you get close to Urinal you shrink. Anything that comes close to Urinal shrinks. Moonlings shrink, spaceships shrink, asteroids shrink, everything shrinks. There are over three million Urinals living on Urinal."

"And you say they've got Jambo?"

"Yes. This is worrying, very worrying."

"Are they violent?"

"Oh yes, very!"

"Then we've got to save him! Can you do that? Can you save him?"

"We could, but it would be very risky. Alternatively we could destroy Urinal once and for all."

"But Jambo? You can't just destroy a planet and kill Jambo!"

"We could, but we won't. They have broken rule 46B section 3C, appendix ccciii point 17."

"What's that?"

"It is the rule that precedes rule 46B section 3C, appendix ccciii point 16."

"Which is?"

"We promise never to visit another planet, especially Earth."

"Urinals must *not* leave their planet. They are an evil and depraved race. Let me show you Earthlings how disgusting these creatures are."

With that, the Man in the Moon clicked his fingers and a screen appeared before them.

"I warn you, they are hideous to look at and may upset your weak Human stomachs."

Terry and Jeremy braced themselves ready for a shock. The Man in the Moon made a strange, low noise and a picture of a Urinal appeared. Terry and Jeremy couldn't believe their eyes. They wanted to say something but tried hard to resist. They looked at each other with puzzled looks on their faces.

"Revolting aren't they?" said the Man in the Moon with disgust in his voice.

"Erm," said Terry.

"Erm indeed," said the Man in the Moon, "They are as evil inside as they are ugly on the outside."

"But..."

"What?"

Jeremy was gesturing to Terry not to say any more but Terry couldn't help himself.

"They look exactly like Moonlings."

The Man in the Moon looked as though he was about to explode.

"Like Moonlings! Like Moonlings! They're nothing like Moonlings!"

"But they've got orange bodies, plate-like heads, tiny black eyes and a thin black line for a mouth. Just like Moonlings."

"Look at their eyes you ignorant Earthling! Can't you see?"

"See what?"

"How different they are."

"No."

"Look again. Look at the screen again, then look at one of the Moonling guards. What do you notice?"

Terry looked and looked and gazed and peered and looked again. Eventually he just shook his head and whispered, "Sorry."

"Humans!! It is perfectly clear that Moonlings have black eyes with a 46 darkness rating. Now, if you look at the Urinals — if you can bear to look — they have very dark grey eyes that are only a 43 darkness rating. Revolting!"

"I see," said Terry, not really seeing at all.

"Oh yes," said Jeremy, also not really seeing at all.

Chapter 11

A Brief History of the Urinals

The following comes from a computerised record from Moonling Central Library:

- In 10000100100 (Moon Years) a group of Moonlings led by Shshshshth led a revolt against the Man in the Moon.
- They were revolting against the Man in the Moon and his government because the government was proposing to stop the mining of cheese from the Moon's inner crust, which they believed was becoming dangerously thin.
- Shshshshth attempted to take power during an eclipse.
- The revolutionaries failed to overthrow the government and were banished to the planet Urinal.
- They were no longer allowed to refer to themselves as Moonlings and were re-named Urinals.
- A government statute was made banning the Urinals from ever making any form of transport that could be used to travel to other planets.

- Any Urinal attempting to leave the planet would be sentenced to death.
- The colour of the Urinals eyes had changed to dark grey 43 darkness-rating due to different conditions on the planet Urinal.

Chapter 12

The Rescue Begins – TOMMOROW!

The Man in the Moon looked sombre. He knew the course of action he must follow.

"We must destroy Urinal! They have breached the law. It saddens me greatly but there is no option. Tomorrow will see the end of Urinal!"

"But what about Jambo?"

"Ah yes, Jambo. That's a shame."

"But you can't just kill him! He's done no harm to you. We've got to save him!"

"Why?"

"Because he's my friend."

"Exactly, someone else who stares up at us. That's probably why the Urinals abducted him; for staring up at *them*."

"But you said their planet is the size of a pinhead. How is anyone going to see it through a telescope?"

"They wouldn't, but *they* could see *him*!"

"It's still not right. You can't just murder a Human Being! That would make you worse than the Urinals."

"Nothing is worse than the Urinals! But, you have pleaded well for your friend. We will try to rescue him. We will leave tomorrow."

"We need to leave now! Why leave it until tomorrow?"

"We cannot leave today."

"Why?"

"Look outside."

Terry peered through a window in the office. The city was completely packed full of Moonlings. There was just a huge sea of blue, red and white shuffling along the paths and roads as well as they could manage, without being knocked down or barged into. Terry noticed that all the Moonlings were wearing scarves and hats, either red or blue.

"What's going on?" he asked.

"That's why we can't go today. We'd never get anywhere and no-one would be willing to come with us if we could. It's Derby Day."

"Derby Day?"

"The Moonchester Derby. Moonchester United versus Moonchester City."

"You're kidding me, right?"

"No. As you've seen with the shops and everything, the Moonlings are fascinated by the way you Earthlings live and we've taken up a lot of your ways of life. Now, you must be hungry. My guards will help you out the back where the streets won't be so crowded. Tomorrow we will try to save your friend."

Terry was led out and taken to MoonDonalds where he ordered some chips. Strangely, the Moonling serving him gave him a small cone full of 'microchips'. Even stranger was the fact that they tasted exactly like proper chips. He just assumed that sometimes the Moonlings got a bit muddled when trying to copy things on Earth.

Once he'd eaten and had something to drink, he was taken back to the Moon Building and was shown to a sparsely-furnished but large bedroom. He slunk down on the bed and rested his head against the incredibly soft, light pillow. Within seconds he was asleep. It had certainly been a tiring and hectic day. He could have slept for hours, but he didn't.

He didn't because a loud whistle and the almost deafening sound of a mass crowd startled him out of his sleep. The noise was coming directly from the inside of his head and without even opening his eyes he could picture the football match that was being played. He didn't know it at the time, but the Moonlings had assumed that he would want to watch the Derby and had organised for the game to be transmitted directly into his brain. At the moment he just wished that he could at least turn the volume down. There was a goal. The noise got louder. He tried burying his head in the pillow but of course this had no effect as the noise was internal.

"Aaagh! Be quiet!! Be quiet!!"

As he spoke the volume went down. He spoke again. The volume went down further. Eventually the sound was hardly audible so Terry only had the images in his head; this he didn't mind. In fact he got quite engrossed in the game in the end.

Just for the record, Moonchester United won 2 – 1 with Wayne Mooney getting the winner.

Chapter 13

I haven't written a chapter 13 because it's an unlucky
number and I'm superstitious!

Chapter 14

The Day After Derby Day

Next morning there was a most peculiar atmosphere (who said there was no atmosphere on the Moon?) Half the Moonlings were almost skipping around and smiling, as well as they could with their long, slim mouths. The other half were walking around like Zombies, their heads hanging down and their mouths seemingly upside down. They clearly took the Derby very seriously!

Today though, Terry's thoughts weren't on the match; all he could think about was Jambo. Before long one of the guards had appeared at the door and asked Terry to follow him. He was taken swiftly to see the Man in the Moon.

"Sit down!" ordered the Man in the Moon. "Today we are preparing to launch 'Operation Jambo'. I have selected a crew of eight of our finest Space Jumpers to infiltrate Urinal and locate and re-capture your friend. They leave in approximately three Lunar Bites, that's about one hour Earth time."

"I want to go!" blurted out Terry.

"You? You? How can you go? Are you a Space Jumper?

Have you been to Space Jumper college? You couldn't possibly go, it would be too dangerous anyway."

"But he's my friend. Teach me to Space Jump."

"Teach you? You Earthlings just get stupider and stupider. It takes a Moonling, a being several thousand times more intelligent than any Human, over five Earth years to train to become a qualified Space Jumper and you think you can learn just like that. You really are priceless!"

"What about taking me with them then?"

"With them? With them? "

"Yes, with them!"

"Well …"

"Aha, it's possible isn't it?"

"Well…"

"Isn't it?"

"Ok, yes, theoretically, but…"

"No buts! He's my friend. If it's possible then I'll do it. Get me ready."

"Alright, alright, I guess you could be useful, especially as you know him so well."

"That's settled then. I guess I'll need a spacesuit or something."

"No."

"No? But surely I can't just travel through space as I am."

"Well, you could brush your hair and tuck your shirt in; you are a bit of a scruffbag if you don't mind me saying."

"I do mind actually! I mean, surely I'll need some special equipment; breathing apparatus, oxygen and stuff. And how can I go down as a Human?"

"Sorry, I was forgetting how backward you Earthlings are. No, all you need is a chip."

"A chip? Do you mean a microchip?"

"Well I'm hardly likely to mean a crinkle-cut potato chip, am I? I'll have my men take you back down to MoonDonalds. They'll know which chip you'll need. Oh, and the going down as a Human bit doesn't matter because there are quite a lot of Humans on Urinal," he added very matter-of-factly.

"Humans? How? Why?"

"The Urinals keep them as pets. Now, we must get on."

So off he was led. The guards ordered the desired chip for him.

"Do you want fries with that?"

"No thanks, just the chip and a Moonling Milkshake to wash it down with."

The chip and the shake soon appeared and Terry was told to swallow the microchip. Strangely it tasted just like a normal Earth chip. He now wished he'd put some salt and vinegar on it. It also seemed to fill him up which was surprising considering the tiny size of it.

Terry was then taken off in a hover cab to a massive, multi-turreted building made from some kind of dazzling white stone or marble. It was almost too bright for Terry's eyes. One of the guards passed him some special, anti-dazzle, wraparound glasses. As Terry slipped them on though, he became immediately aware that they weren't just anti-dazzle, they were anti-sight (or in other words, he couldn't see a flippin' thing!). The glasses clamped tightly to his head as he tried to remove them.

"You are not permitted to see any more until we are inside the Jumping Zone. This is a high security area," announced one of the Moonling guards, full of his own self-importance. "Only top-level Government workers are allowed to see this installation."

'Twonk!' thought Terry.

They exited the hover cab and he was led, still blindfolded, through a multitude of passageways, up stairs and through a number of sliding electronic doors. It seemed that they were walking miles. At last they stopped and Terry felt the glasses loosen around his head. They were slowly and gently removed. As Terry's eyes adjusted to the light he could see that he was inside a very small and very empty room. The entire room was purple and there was not a seat to be seen. Even the guards had vanished. He just stood in the middle of this room alone. His heart started beating much faster as he become increasingly anxious. Where was he? Why wasn't there anybody else here? Was it a trap? Was this the end? Was that the end of all the questions for now?

It was. The room had become cold; really cold; icy cold! Suddenly Terry felt frozen to the spot. He couldn't even move his mouth. Suddenly, eight Moonlings appeared from nowhere. They stood in a row of four either side of Terry. The nearest two Moonlings linked their arms round Terry's legs and began swinging gently backwards and forwards. In front of them a small, white circle appeared on one of the purple walls. Gradually the circle became bigger and bigger and they were able to look out into space. Terry could just about make out a couple of the planets and a few stars. The Moonlings walked forward towards the ever increasing circle, carrying Terry along with them. Their speed suddenly increased as they shot forward and vaulted out through the white circle. They were flying, or floating, or both. They were speeding through space but Terry hardly felt like he was moving. He could still not move, apart from a slight swivel of his eyes. The Moonlings were gripping firmly onto his legs. It was hurting now but this was actually reassuring to Terry.

They continued through space, maintaining what felt like a reasonably straight path forward. It all felt so effortless. Suddenly though, Terry started to feel different; smaller. That was it, smaller! He felt as though his whole body was being squeezed inwards. He also found that he had regained some of his movement and he looked to his side to see that the Moonlings were also shrinking at an alarming rate.

Thump! They stopped. They stopped very quickly. They stopped with a bang. They'd landed. They were on the planet Urinal. Operation Jambo was about to begin.

Chapter 15

Urinal

Terry looked around. Not for the first time, he was very disappointed. It was very similar to the Moon except that the rock had a slight yellowy hue to it. 'Is this it?' he thought to himself.

"Is this it?" he asked the Moonling Space Jumpers.

"Yes. This is Urinal."

"So where is everyone?"

"Inside of course!" Terry didn't think the guard really needed to add the 'of course', or the tut, or the sarcasm in his voice.

"So how do we get in?"

"How? How?"

"Yes, how?"

"Through the door of course! You Earthlings!!!"

Terry was not warming to his new colleagues. He was soon warming however as the Moonling Space

Jumpers discovered a door hatch and lifted it open. The heat poured out of the gap.

"We can't go in there! It's boiling!"

"Drink this." They offered him a small vessel of liquid. It was so cold that it almost burnt his tongue. He could feel it cooling his whole body as he swallowed it. The hot blast from the hatch became little more than a slightly uncomfortable warmth. The Moonlings passed through the hatch and Terry followed. The interior was a wild mixture of reds, yellows and oranges, constantly changing pattern and shape. The colours seemed to be formed from a mixture of gases, some producing sparks of electricity.

Down below them, a very long way below them, was the outline of a massive city. Everything appeared to be yellow lots of different shades of yellow, but yellow nonetheless. As yet they could see no sign of life.

"Put in these lenses, we must make our eyes appear to be a 43 darkness-rating like the Urinals. As disgusting as it is, we must suffer this grave embarrassment if we are to be able to save your friend. All fixed? Then let us begin the descent."

They stood on a circular platform, very similar to that found on the Moon, and slowly descended towards the city below. There were at least forty Urinals spread around the platform. They still looked the same as

Moonlings to Terry. He didn't say anything. He knew how important it was to be careful and not to bring attention to themselves.

"They still look like Moonlings to me," he whispered (not very quietly) to one of the Space Jumpers. The Space Jumper just glared at him Terry was not good at keeping quiet. He never had been.

Chapter 16

The Search Begins in Earnest

As they reached the floor and shuffled off the platform, Terry looked around him. Everything was yellow; everything. Everything that is, apart from the Urinals. He was also quick to note that the streets were far less busy than they had been in Moonchester. There was also a smell. It was not a nice smell. In fact, thought Terry, it really stinks! He'd smelt something like it before but he couldn't quite put his finger on it. In fact, he wasn't sure that he'd want to put his finger on it!

"What is that smell?" he asked one of the Space Jumpers.

"Cheese," he replied.

"Cheese?"

"Cheese."

That's it, that's where he'd smelt it before, his Grandad! No, not his actual Grandad! His Grandad was a lover of blue cheese, that horrible mouldy stuff! That was the smell.

"It's gross! Why does it stink of mouldy cheese?"

"Because it's *made* from mouldy cheese of course!"

"What? The whole planet?"

"Yes, but it is particularly strong here in Earnest."

"Earnest?"

"Yes, this is the city of Earnest. Didn't you read the title to this chapter?"

"The Search Begins in Earnest? That's awful!"

"Yes. Now be quiet or someone will become suspicious."

They moved stealthily across the road and entered a large building that appeared to be empty. Once inside, one of the Space Jumpers (Mimomimomi if you're interested) led them through a dark passage-way and into a side room. Once inside he closed the door behind them. It appeared that he was the designated leader of the group.

"Ok, we are going to have to split up. There are too many of us to travel around together without raising suspicion. As you have noticed, the population on Urinal is much smaller than that in the Moon and the Urinals tend to be less sociable. They are also more dangerous and potentially violent, especially towards Moonlings. Intelligence has informed us that Jambo is being held in the Urethra Parliamentary

Quarters. This is quite some distance from here and is heavily guarded. I suggest that we meet up at an area known as 'The Flush' which is just on the outskirts of Urethra. We will re-assemble there and consider our next move."

He then handed out a watch to each of the group.

"This contains a navigation device that will transmit the directions directly to your brain. Directions have been pre-set and will take you on different routes but will eventually lead to the same destination. Terry, I want you to come with me."

Terry just nodded. He was impressed by Mimomimomi.

The pair headed eastwards along the side of the winding, yellow road. They passed shops, hotels, restaurants, bars and night clubs. There was an atmosphere Terry didn't like. It wasn't obvious, but he felt uncomfortable. Despite everything being some shade of yellow, it all seemed dirty – run down. The Urinals themselves appeared to be just milling around as if they were waiting for something. They were constantly looking around, their tiny dark grey (shade 43) eyes peering anxiously about them; anxious and yet menacing at the same time. Terry and Mimomimomi tried to replicate their behaviour as they continued on their way.

'Turn right at the next junction' came the next message from the navigation system. They did as instructed and found themselves walking down a very narrow and dark yellow passage. There was a group of over-flowing dustbins and masses of litter blowing around the floor. Suddenly Terry slipped and almost fell. He checked his shoe. It smelt. It smelt badly. REALLY BADLY!

"What is it?" he asked.

"Urinals have pets," was the short answer from Mimomimomi.

"Yuk."

Terry managed to find a piece of cloth which he dipped into one of the many yellow puddles in the road and did his best to clean his shoe.

"This place sucks!" he announced.

"Quiet!" ordered Mimomimomi.

"No wonder it's called Urinal," Terry mumbled to himself.

Chapter 17

Shshshshth The 15th, Pets and the Destruction of the Urf

On they went, led forward by the Sat Nav. The further they walked, the worse the area seemed to become. Houses were boarded up, doors were broken, litter was strewn everywhere. The Urinals also seemed more and more seedy; desperate. Several of them were laid down by the side of the road, others were sitting on their doorsteps swigging from bottles of thick, gloopy liquid. The Sat Nav was certainly not taking them by the tourist route – if there was such a thing on Urinal.

A bottle smashed behind them. Terry turned to see two Urinals fighting amongst the litter on the floor. Yellow blood was pouring from the face of one of them. Terry could feel his heart racing and a feeling of increasing anxiety building up inside him. He turned back, eager to keep within close distance of Mimomimomi, but the road ahead was empty! Where was he?

Suddenly, Terry felt an icy blast from behind him. He couldn't move. It was as though his whole body had been frozen. It had! He could barely see anything out of his misty, icy eyes. He felt somebody push him from behind and then felt himself being lifted forwards. His whole body was frozen stiff in the position he'd been standing in. He tried to see where he was being taken but his vision was all but blocked. The only movement he could feel in his entire body was his heart beating ever faster; he was worried it might burst if it didn't slow down soon.

On and on he was carried until finally he could just about make out a large building in front of him. They seemed to take him inside, presumably through the door (after opening it of course!). They carried him through a little further and then upwards, seemingly via a flight of stairs. At last they laid him down. Slowly, some feeling began to come back to him. He felt as though he was being de-frosted. He was. The warmth gradually thawed him and some feeling came back into his limbs. His eyes began to de-mist and he could start to make out shapes in front of him. Eventually he could see and move freely; freely that is, within the confines of his container. The back and side walls were white and solid whilst the front was made mainly of a transparent material that seemed very similar to glass. Terry also noticed that he was slowly rotating inside the container. It was almost as though he was standing inside a large microwave oven (again, this was because this was exactly what he was doing). The floor stopped revolving and Terry heard a loud 'pinging' noise from outside. Then the door flipped open.

Terry warily pushed the door forward and looked out. In front of him was a group of some twenty Urinals all dressed in black military-style uniforms and peaked caps. The welcoming committee did not look in the least bit like they were actually going to welcome him. He gulped, nearly tripped, and tried to talk.

"SILENCE!" boomed a voice from the middle of the group before Terry could actually make a sound. One of the Urinals stepped forward. This Urinal was different though. This Urinal really did have different eyes. They were black, but somehow more than black. They weren't just a darker shade to the other Urinals or indeed to the Moonlings, these were of a darkness that was beyond colour and had something more like *depth* to them; an almost infinite depth. They were not friendly eyes.

Terry could hardly bare to look into them for fear that he might somehow be drawn into them and devoured.

"Look at me Earthling! Look at me! Dare you turn away from the Great Shshshshth the 15th? Dare you?"

Terry looked at him, his whole body shaking with fear.

"There is somebody here that I'm sure you'd like to meet."

In through a door at the side of the room was led a Human. Two guards marched him forwards towards Terry. He looked very pale and sickly, and his eyes were red and swollen. Even so, Terry could still recognise him.

"Jambo!"

"Terry!"

"What a lovely, touching reunion!" mocked Shshshshth the 15th. Now, please take a seat."

Seats were thrust roughly beneath Terry and Jambo. In front of them a huge screen appeared on the bright yellow wall. It was an image of Earth.

"Recognise it?" asked Shshshshth the 15th (I'll call him 15th from now on as the s,t and h on my keyboard are starting to wear out!)

The two boys both nodded.

"Well, keep looking Humans because this will be the last time you see it."

"Are you going to kill us?" asked Terry.

"Oh no, we'll keep you, you're worth good money as pets. Oh no, it's not *you* we're going to destroy, it's your *planet*. Today we destroy Earth!"

"But you can't!" began Terry and Jambo almost together, "our families live there. You can't just decide to destroy Earth! You can't!"

"Oh, but I can! And I will! The Moonlings banished us to this planet and banned us from taking pets from other planets. These pets are our lives; they have great meaning to us. Earthlings are the most sought after pets of all, but it was made illegal to visit Earth and any Urinal found guilty of Human-Snatching faces immediate death. Only the bravest or most desperate Urinals dare to break this law. Many hundreds have been mercilessly killed. But today everything changes. Today we will destroy their precious Earth. If *we* cannot use Earth then we will make sure that *nobody* can. NOBODY!"

Terry was almost expecting a long, evil, demented laugh to follow.

"Ha, ha, ha, ha, ha, ha, ha, ha, ha, ha, ha, ha, ha, ha, ha, ha, ha, haa, haa, haaa, haaaaaaa!" laughed the 15th in an evil and demented way.

"But you can't!"

"Tape their mouths!"

Their mouths were forcefully taped up.

"Now sit back and enjoy! You may wave goodbye! Ha, ha, haa, haa etc."

Jambo and Terry shuffled in their seats but found themselves unable to rise. Somehow they'd been stuck down. They both wrestled frantically but only succeeded in almost toppling their chairs. They were helpless. Earth was about to be destroyed. *Their* Earth, *their* families, *their* friends, and millions of innocent Humans were about to be destroyed. All life on Earth was about to be destroyed! And all Terry and Jambo could do was sit and watch!

The 15th flicked a switch and a countdown began at the top of the big screen. 1:00 Earth minute, 00:59, 00:58, 00:57, 00:56 Earth seconds but for Terry and Jambo they seemed to be nano-seconds. Soon everything they held dear, *everything* they knew, just everything would be gone. 00:33, 00:32, 00:31. Down it went. Down, down, down. 00:10, 00:09, 00:08. Surely this was where somebody stormed in and saved the day. All those films that Terry had watched; always there was a hero arriving just in the nick of time. 00:05, 00:04, 00:03. Where was the hero? Where was Superman? Spiderman? Something man?

Suddenly the door crashed open and in flew the Space Jumpers led by Mimomimomi. They were 'seriously' armed and had very quickly blasted away most of the Urinals. The 15th was soon the only Urinal standing. The Space Jumpers directed their weapons at him. He was trapped. He was going to die, or be captured and imprisoned. None of this seemed to be bothering him as his liquorice-like mouth turned into a wide smile. Behind him, on the huge screen, there was a massive explosion. Time had run out. Earth was blown into tiny parts.

"I win!" he shouted as he stormed forwards towards the Space Jumpers. They all fired off their weapons at the same time and the 15th, still smiling, collapsed in a heap on the floor.

Chapter 18

Saved... But Too Late

Mimomimomi and the other Space Jumpers helped to release Terry and Jambo from their seats. Both the boys were sobbing violently and could barely believe what they'd just seen.

"Come on, we need to be quick."

"But it's too late..." answered Terry through floods of tears, "too late!"

"Just come!"

Terry and Jambo were both pulled from their seats, then taken out of the room and were soon speeding through the streets of Urinal towards the circular platform that would lead them up to the surface. They jumped onto the platform just as it was about to leave the ground and did their best not to make themselves too conspicuous. This was difficult with Terry and Jambo still sobbing loudly. The Urinals around them didn't really take a lot of notice though and they soon reached the top and exited through the hatch and onto the surface. The Space Jumpers, with Jambo and Terry between them, linked up and positioned themselves ready to jump. They stood in a line, barely moving except to make very fine adjustments. Suddenly, an ear-splitting alarm went off behind them and the hatch flew open, pouring Urinal guards onto the surface. They'd been spotted! They'd been found out! The guards raised their weapons and prepared to fire but the Space Jumpers jumped just in time. The speed was extraordinary and Terry felt that he was going to explode any minute. They began to spin; they began to spin very fast! This was not how it had been on their way to Urinal; this was frightening; this was wrong!

They began to slow. The spinning was less violent. In front of them they could see the Moon, shining brightly from the sun's rays. They slowed still further until they were almost gliding. The landing was smooth; so smooth that they all landed upright on their feet. They were safe; dazed, but safe.

Soon they were surrounded and then escorted away in hover cars by Moonling security guards. Terry and Jambo were placed into the back, still shaken by their journey through space. They soon arrived at their destination and were ushered inside the large building and escorted into the Man in The Moon's office. His face beamed as he saw them.

"Welcome back! So our mission was successful, as always."

"But..." began Terry.

"The Urinals are beaten again and you have both been saved. What a glorious day! We must celebrate!"

"Celebrate? Celebrate? Are you mad? What about Earth? Glorious day? Earth is destroyed, all my friends and family have been killed and you want to throw some kind of party!" shouted Terry, with steam coming out of his ears.

"What?"

"You don't know?"

"Don't know what?"

"That Earth has been destroyed!"

"Oh yes, brilliant don't you think?"

Terry was boiling with anger and looked ready to fly at the Man in the Moon. Two armed guards noticed and stood in front of him.

"Brilliant!" screamed Terry, trying to pass the guards. What do you mean, brilliant?"

"It was so clever to let them destroy Urf."

"Clever! Clever? And it's Earth, not Urf you bubble-headed freak."

"No, it's Urf... You don't understand do you? Has no one told you? Urf was destroyed."

"I know; I used to live there. I watched it blow up. I watched all my friends and family being destroyed."

"They can't have been there, we only built Urf yesterday."

"Made it? Made it? Have you gone mad? And it's Earth, ok, Earth!!!"

"No, it's Urf. Yesterday we created a planet of a similar size to Earth and placed it directly in line with Earth from Urinal. The Urinals believe that they have destroyed Earth but they've actually only destroyed Urf, an uninhabited planet that we created yesterday."

"You created a planet?"

"Yes, Urf."

"In one day?" Terry was staggered.

"So Earth is ok?"

"Of course it is. We wouldn't let anything happen to Earth. Without Earthlings we wouldn't have any pets."

"Pets? You mean that you keep humans as pets too?"

"Oh yes, we love them."

"And you just come down and take them?"

"Oh no. Not live ones. We're only allowed to take ones that have recently died; usually those that have died young, we prefer those. You see, when a human lives out their full life they go off to Heaven or Hell depending on how they've lived their lives. Those who die early have to go through a really complex sorting process. While their cases are being decided, Moonlings are allowed to bring them up to the Moon and keep them as pets. Once the decision is made, off they go!"

"Are you taking the ..."

"Oh no. The Urinals do that but we don't! The Urinals take live humans, against the law of course. Most of the humans on the Missing Persons' Register have actually been taken by Urinals."

Not for the first, or even second time, Terry could hardly believe what he was hearing.

Chapter 19

So What Now?

"So what happens now?" Terry asked.

"Well," said the Man in the Moon, "I guess we'd better be letting you get off back to Earth. You and Jambo."

"Just like that?"

"Just like that. Sort of. Obviously we've got to completely wipe your memory of anything and everything that's happened to you in the last few days since we brought you up here."

"Obviously. Is that really necessary? We won't tell anybody, will we Jambo?" Jambo shook his head in agreement.

"Of course you wouldn't. We know how incredibly honest and trustworthy you Humans are. Of course you wouldn't tell anyone, at least not until you opened your mouths."

"I had always thought that even if other forms of life existed, Humans would almost certainly be the only ones to understand and use sarcasm, but I have to hand it to you, you run us very close."

"Sorry Terry, you may be the most honest and honourable Human Being ever, but unfortunately that still means that you would be sure to go blabbing about your whole experience within 48 Earth hours. Wiping the memories will only take us about 15 Earth minutes."

"Okay, I guess, but wait a minute. What about Jeremy?"

"Ah, yes... Jeremy."

"Yes, Jeremy."

"Well he'll be staying with us."

"But you can't hold him up here against his will, that would make you as bad as the Urinals."

"We're not holding him against his will; he has agreed to teach us."

"Teach you? Teach you what? He's an idiot."

"To you maybe, but to us he's 'Special'"

"He's *special* alright! How can a super-intelligent race like yours, that can create a whole planet in one day and can space-jump from one planet to another, believe that Jeremy is anything other than an annoying pain in the backside with a severe case of verbal diarrhoea?"

"It is right that we can do many great things. In many ways we are far superior to Humans but Jeremy has knowledge of things beyond Science. He speaks of emotions, of love, of jealousy; things that we know little of. To us it is fascinating."

"Each to their own I guess. Won't his family miss him though?"

Just then Jeremy walked into the room.

"I have no family Terry. My parents died when I was young and I have never found a life partner or soul mate."

For once Terry managed to keep his thoughts to himself, 'Life partner! Soul mate! No wonder he's single.'

"I see," said Terry, "So you're happy to stay?"

"I insist upon it dude. They really seem to appreciate me up here. I often felt that I wasn't really respected or wanted on Earth?

"Really? But..." Terry couldn't complete the sentence. He wasn't a good liar.

"Goodbye Terry, goodbye Jambo, hang loose guys."

Terry and Jambo shook his hand and that of the Man in the Moon, and were then escorted away to have their memories 'tidied up' and then to be transported back to Earth.

Chapter 20

Back to Urf, Sorry, Earth

Terry looked around his room. The Zestron Star SX80 had returned and sat on its tripod still pointed up through the skylight. He lifted himself up from his bed and wiped his eyes. Had he fallen asleep? There was a knock at the door and then Perry (Terry's older brother if you've forgotten by now) came barging in and immediately started to poke fun at Terry.

"Hi Little Bro, still looking for the little green men then? Got anything to eat? I'm starving. Got any Mars bars, or Star bars or Milky Ways or a bit of Galaxy perhaps?"

"Shut up Perry, you're not funny."

"New telescope?"

"Yes, it's the Zestron Star SX80."

"Wow!" Perry said sarcastically, "it's like living with Doctor Who."

"Just clear off will you!"

"Ok, ok, calm down Little Bro. Just don't go stargazing too long, I don't want you screaming out in your sleep about the Man in the Moon or Moonlings again tonight."

"What?"

"Last night. You don't even remember do you? Dad had to come in and see if you were alright."

"Did he?"

"Oh yeah, and then you started babbling on about Mimimimimi or something. What a nut!" Perry added as he left.

Moonlings? Man in the Moon? For some reason these things rang a bell with Terry, it was almost as if … He moved over to his telescope and looked directly towards the moon. It was a full moon tonight. He smiled to himself. Of course *Moonlings* meant some-thing to him; of course the *Man in the Moon* rang a bell. He remembered everything; Urinal, Shshshshth the 15th, The Moonchester Derby, Mimimimimi; he remembered it all. The Man in the Moon was right, the Moonlings may be a superior race but they weren't so clever when it came to Human feelings and certainly not about memories. Yes, his, and Jambo's, memories had been wiped but as soon as he looked back up through his telescope all the memories just flooded back into his brain.

The Man in the Moon had been wrong about another thing too. Terry and Jambo kept the whole adventure between themselves. Or at least they did for a couple of weeks. THEN THEY TOLD ME!!